T0381186

MATTHEW THE NEW YORKER

DENNIS TEALL SR.

WESTBOW
PRESS®
A DIVISION OF THOMAS NELSON
& ZONDERVAN

Copyright © 2024 Dennis Teall Sr.

All rights reserved. No part of this book may be used or reproduced by
any means, graphic, electronic, or mechanical, including photocopying,
recording, taping or by any information storage retrieval system
without the written permission of the author except in the case
of brief quotations embodied in critical articles and reviews.

WestBow Press books may be ordered through
booksellers or by contacting:

WestBow Press
A Division of Thomas Nelson & Zondervan
1663 Liberty Drive
Bloomington, IN 47403
www.westbowpress.com
844-714-3454

Because of the dynamic nature of the Internet, any web
addresses or links contained in this book may have changed
since publication and may no longer be valid. The views
expressed in this work are solely those of the author and do
not necessarily reflect the views of the publisher, and the
publisher hereby disclaims any responsibility for them.

Any people depicted in stock imagery provided by Getty Images are
models, and such images are being used for illustrative purposes only.
Certain stock imagery © Getty Images.

Scripture quotations marked KJV are from the Holy Bible,
King James Version (Authorized Version). First published
in 1611. Quoted from the KJV Classic Reference Bible,
Copyright © 1983 by The Zondervan Corporation.

ISBN: 979-8-3850-2530-5 (sc)
ISBN: 979-8-3850-2532-9 (e)

Library of Congress Control Number: 2024909578

Print information available on the last page.

WestBow Press rev. date: 10/29/2024

This book is dedicated to those who have inspired me in so many ways, Jack Wright, Barbra Baker, and so many others.
I hope this story inspires others to come to know Jesus Christ as I have.

A NOTE TO THE READER

While this book is set in and around the town of North Platte, Nebraska, the characters are fictional. There is no intended resemblance between any character and me, even though I grew up in North Platte and some of my time there is woven into the story.

The mobile home court referred to in the story did not exist in 1970. The gas station and garage on the corner of Fourth and Jeffers has been replaced with a pharmacy. I did own a 1963 Chevy Bel Air station wagon, and yes, Hinky Dinky's really was a grocery store back then.

I hope you enjoy the story. My greatest and heartfelt desire is to bring people to know Christ Jesus as their Lord and Savior.

CHAPTER 1

Matthew looked out the window as the plane taxied up to the terminal at Lee Bird Field. He was surprised at how small the airport was compared to the ones that he had encountered while in the military.

Instead of a jet bridge being connected to the side of the plane, a set of steps was wheeled up to off-load passengers. As he entered the terminal, he took notice of the restaurant to his right, which was more of a coffee shop, and the small area for baggage claim just inside the door on his left. The terminal was small, and there were no large crowds of people rushing about as there would have been in a large airport. Only three people had got off the plane, and four were waiting to get on. There was only one person working the ticket counter instead of five or six, and the only airline sign he saw was Frontier.

To the right of the front doors was a Hertz rental car counter, again with only one person working. He didn't want to rent a car because if he did, he would have to bring it back, and then he would need to find another way back into town later on. He had arrived wearing his US Army dress greens and would need some civvies. He had several other errands to run as he settled in.

After collecting his luggage, he walked outside expecting to find a taxi. Where there would normally be half dozen or so, he found none. He went back inside and asked the girl at the Hertz counter how he could get a cab.

She pointed to several telephone handsets on the wall opposite the front doors. Most of the handsets were for motels and hotels. He located the receiver that indicated it was for a taxi and picked it up. After a short wait, a woman answered with a direct question: "Where do you want to go?"

Matthew explained he was at the airport, to

which she replied, "I know where you are. Where do you wish to be taken?"

"Into town," he said, adding that he was new to the area and wasn't sure if there were any hotels near the downtown area.

"Cab will be there in ten minutes."

Matthew went back outside and waited for the cab to show up. There were patches of snow still on the ground, and it was overcast. A cold wind blew across him. This was the second week of March 1970.

CHAPTER

2

Fifteen minutes later, the cab that he had been waiting for finally arrived. After loading his luggage, he explained to the driver that he wanted a hotel as close to the downtown as he could get.

The driver said his name was Jim. He took Matthew to the Pawnee Hotel downtown. After checking in, he bought a newspaper and went up to his room. While looking through the ads, he came across a mobile home with two bedrooms for rent. He called the number listed and talked with a woman who said her name was Jackie. He inquired whether the mobile home was still available. If so, he would be interested in it. She said it was.

He called for another ride and told the woman at the cab company exactly where he wanted to go. Then he went out to wait in front of the hotel.

Jim showed up again and took Matthew to the trailer court, which was just south of the railroad tracks on the west end of town. "Would you mind waiting for me, Jim?" Matthew asked.

"I can wait," Jim said, "but I will have to keep the meter running."

Matthew said that would be okay. He entered the office and was met by a friendly older woman who, he figured, was in her forties. He explained that he had come to see about the mobile home that was for rent, and Jackie took him down to look at it.

The front door opened into a living room, and to the right was a bathroom with a front bedroom. To his left and past the living room was the kitchen. The laundry area was by the back door, and on down the hallway was a second bathroom and a back bedroom. There was also a carport attached to the side of the mobile home.

Matthew said that the mobile home would work just fine for him. Jackie told him what the rent was. She would need two months' deposit, considering he was young and just out of the service. Based on her experiences with previous renters, she wanted extra security in case any partying got out of hand or the renter skipped out in the middle of the night.

They returned to the office, and he filled out his information on a rental contract. He explained that he was new to the area. He was hoping to find a good used car and a job while making North Platte his home. He put down the money for the deposit and the first month's rent. He got his receipt and the keys and said, "I will start moving in tomorrow."

Once he was back in the cab, they headed back toward town. Matthew asked Jim if he knew where he might find a good used car.

"A friend of mine mentioned a station wagon for sale," Jim said. "He thought I might be interested in it. I can take you there, if that would be something that would work for you?"

"As long as it's reliable," Matthew said.

Jim took him to the northwest corner of Fourth and Jeffers Streets, where there was a gas station with a garage out back. Jim pulled up to the garage and pointed out the station wagon.

They both got out and went inside. Jim talked to one of the mechanics and introduced Matthew.

The mechanic, whose name was Tom, said that the motor had been rebuilt and was in good condition.

They went out to look the station wagon over. Matthew told Jim he could go on ahead and leave. He could walk back to the hotel if he needed to, since it was only a few blocks away. After paying for his ride, he went to check out the car.

It was a 1963 Chevy Bel Air station wagon with a white exterior and a blue interior. It had cloth seats and a 283 engine under the hood. The tires still had a lot of tread left on them. The car was clean with no visible damage nor any signs of rust.

Tom said the owner, who also owned the garage, was asking $750 for it. "Do you want me to go get him?"

"Yes, please," Matthew said. After he talked with the owner, he asked to take the car for a test drive. They climbed in, and after a short drive Matthew said he would take the car.

He handed over the money in cash and signed the paperwork. While he was waiting for the title to be delivered from the courthouse, he walked over to a Triple A office east of the courthouse on Dewey Street. He talked with an insurance agent about getting the car insured and becoming a Triple A member. His granddad had had Triple A insurance along with a membership, and his granddad swore by them.

After leaving the Triple A office. he returned to pick up his car, then drove over to the hotel and parked on the street. He walked over to Johnny's Café on the corner of Sixth and Bailey. It was part of the Trailways bus terminal, and the Greyhound bus depot was on the northeast corner.

CHAPTER 3

After a good night's sleep, Matthew checked out of the hotel, stashing his duffel bag and suitcase in the car along with his carry-on bag. He walked back over to Johnny's Café to have breakfast.

After he finished eating, he drove over to Sears and Roebuck, where he purchased clothes, hangers, kitchen items, dishes, silverware, a coffee maker, and a toaster. Then he added a broom with a dustpan, an ironing board, an iron, a mop and a bucket, a trash can, and a clothes basket. He picked out a washer and dryer for delivery at around one that afternoon.

After he left Sears and Roebuck, he drove over to Whitaker's Furniture, where he purchased a twin bed, a nightstand, a lamp, a kitchen table with two chairs, a recliner, an end table, and a floor lamp, which were to be delivered around two thirty.

Leaving Whitaker's Furniture, he went to Hinky Dinky's, a grocery store, to pick up a few food items such as milk, bread, peanut butter, baloney, mayo, potato chips, coffee, and some pop, along with laundry and dish soap.

He arrived back at the mobile home just before the Sears truck did. While they were installing the washer and dryer, he put stuff away in the kitchen. Then he started removing tags from the clothing so he could get them washed later. He also put items in the utility closet. After the men from Sears left, he started washing clothes. While the clothes were going, he washed up the dishes, and wiped the inside and outside of the cupboards and the counters.

When the truck from Whitaker's arrived, he helped to carry in the items. After the furniture was in place and the bed put together, the men from Whitaker's left. Matthew finished washing the dishes, made a pot of coffee, and moved clothes from the washer to the dryer. Then he had a peanut butter, baloney, and mayo sandwich with potato chips on the side.

He went back to the Sears store and picked up bedding and a shower curtain. He had been short on time when he picked up groceries, so he stopped by Hinky Dinky's again for a few more items such as butter, sugar, salt, pepper, and meat.

Back at the trailer, he washed up the bedding. Then he made the bed and took a shower. Now that he was finally out of his US Army dress greens, he felt more back into civilian life. He unpacked his suitcase. He had had a box made, now filled with items from his time in the army, which he put in the bottom drawer of the built-in dresser.

The next day he dropped off his military uniforms to the dry cleaners. He then went to Pearson Appliance, where he purchased a stereo system with a record changer and an AM-FM radio. He went to the nearby record store to buy some classical albums. The stereo was delivered that afternoon.

Right after the deliverymen left, there was a knock on the door. His next-door neighbor was standing there.

"I will not tolerate drunken parties or loud music," she said. "And you are also to stay away from my daughter."

Her daughter just happened to be watching out the window, smiling at him.

Matthew stared at the woman at his doorstep and said nothing until she finally left.

He went to First National Bank, where he opened up a checking and savings account. From the bank he went to the courthouse and got his car licensed. He picked up a driver's manual, which he studied over the next couple of days. Matthew continued to pick up items from here and there as he had need of them.

Friday afternoon, he took the driver's test and received a Nebraska driver's license. Matthew spent the weekend looking around town and checking out Maloney Reservoir south of town. He also went out to the Scout's Rest Ranch, which had been built in the 1880s and was the home of William F. Cody, better known as Buffalo Bill.

CHAPTER 4

Monday morning, Matthew was sitting outside the job service, having arrived before it officially opened. When people started showing up, he went in to seek employment.

Matthew was placed with an agent. After he gave the necessary information about himself, the agent made a phone call. After the call, Matthew was given a card to give to the employee he was to contact. He was sent over to the city shops.

After filling out a job application, he was interviewed by Bud, the supervisor in charge of the streets.

Asked when he could start working, Matthew replied, "I am available now."

Matthew was taken over to meet up with three other employees. After all the introductions, he went to work.

The questions began a short time after he was on the job.

"We don't know anyone from here with the last name of McCracken. Did you go to school here?"

Matthew told them about growing up on a farm in Upstate New York, which was the reason for his accent. He was raised by his mother's parents after his folks had been killed. He joined the army when he turned eighteen and spent three years as a field medic. Now that his grandparents were gone, he had come to North Platte to start a new life. He had heard it was a good town to live and grow up in. There was a lot of information that he had left out—details he wasn't ready to share with anyone quite yet.

Toward the end of the week, a snowstorm moved through, and he was commandeered to help plow snow. When they were on the job site, it seemed like he was doing most of the work. He figured it was because he was the new guy. Then the next week when the crew went out, he was still the only one who seemed to be doing most of the work.

The other three guys he was working with were always trying to get him to go to a bar and have a drink with them after work.

Matthew said, "Don't drink, never have, and not about to start now." He didn't add that he wasn't going to let his grandmother down, even though she was no longer living. Drinking alcohol was the one thing Grams always harped about and condemned. He figured that it must have played a part in his mom and dad's death.

The guys said that he could at least come along and join them by having a Coke or something.

To which Matthew said, "I can have the Coke at home."

On Friday he received his first paycheck, which he deposited. He was hoping to save up enough money for a down payment on a house someday.

CHAPTER

5

Monday morning, Bud called him into the office and reassigned him to a pickup with some material and tools, along with a list of projects that needed to be done. He spent that week working by himself. Bud would either tell Matthew what needed to be done or give him a list of tasks that needed taken care of. Sometimes these might include helping others, but mostly he worked alone.

March faded away, and April took over with frequent rain showers. With all the rain they were getting, he broke down and bought an old-style push mover, along with a garden hose and sprinkler for when the rain finally stopped.

The employees he had been working with were complaining to Bud that they were in need of some help. Bud informed them that he had been sitting down the street a ways watching them, and the only one he could ever recall seeing doing any actual work was Matthew. If the three of them would get out of the vehicle and stop just standing around, they wouldn't need anyone else to do the work for them.

They tried to convince the supervisor that he had only been around when Matthew was working, but that they indeed had done their share.

"The department head and myself have been watching for a number of days, and I want to know when you three were ever doing any work in that time frame," Bud said. When they had no answer, he said, "Go and do the work you three have been assigned, or else go home."

The three of them left, blaming Matthew for the situation they had put themselves in. But after watching Matthew work, none of them were willing to confront him about it.

CHAPTER

6

Matthew obtained a library card. He would check out three or four books on Saturday and return them the next Saturday. He relaxed in the evenings and on the weekends by reading or doing crossword puzzles, and by listening to classical music, which he had grown up with.

By mid-April, the weather was nice enough that he would take his coffee and a book outside. Later on he picked up a lawn chair along with an outdoor table, which he put by the side of the mobile home to hold his coffee cup and his book. He read until it got too dark or the weather turned bad.

Some girls from the trailer court had been walking past his trailer from time to time. They would look over his direction and whisper to one another while giggling as they went by. One of the girls who had been walking by off and on finally got brave enough to stop and say hello.

"My name is Amber Marshall," she said. "I live in lot sixteen. My dad works for the FAA out at the airport. My mother's name is Susan. I have two sisters, named Ann and Angie." She continued to talk nonstop for almost forty minutes. Then she asked what his name was.

Matthew told her.

Amber said, "My dad is John, and my mom is Susan. Well, I had better be getting back home before my mother sends my sisters out looking for me."

By time she left, he had been well informed of everyone she knew in the trailer court. She talked about her mom, sisters, grandparents, and other relatives who lived in Michigan. Her folks moved to North Platte when she was three, and she was now sixteen. Her sister Ann was eleven, and Angie was five.

The next time she stopped by was on a Saturday in mid-May, and as before she talked nonstop about school, a boy who wouldn't leave her alone, and how she would be turning seventeen on July first.

Matthew would always put down his book and pay attention to her, listening with delight to everything she had to say as she rattled on. He found her quite entertaining.

She came by more often. Sometimes she would stay just a few minutes, and other times she would chatter on for as long as an hour. It amazed him that she could find so much to talk about. He wondered if it was because she was nervous, or maybe she just had no one else to talk to.

One day she asked to use the bathroom. He told her to use the one toward the back of the trailer. When she came back out, she said, "You don't have much furniture, and those green towels are the ugliest towels I have ever seen. Wherever did you find them?"

"The towels are government issued. And no, I don't have a lot of furniture, beings there is just me. Besides, this place is only temporary until I can find something more permanent, but first I have to save up enough for the down payment, which will take me at least a year or more."

Amber smiled and said, "I best be getting home."

A few days later, when Matthew was sitting outside after supper, Amber came by again. She began asking questions about him, like how old he was, where he worked, and if he graduated from there.

"I am from Upstate New York," Matthew said. "I grew up on a farm with my grandparents after my parents died in a car accident. My mom and dad were going to a meeting in a town nearby, and they left me with my mom's folks. I was only three months old at the time. On the way back from the meeting, my mom and dad were killed in a single car accident.

"My dad's family wanted nothing to do with me. They blamed my mother for their son's death. Grams said they didn't want my dad to marry my mother. They didn't like my mom, and they called her a gold digger. But Mom and Dad got married anyway. My dad was several years older than my mother. I thought maybe Dad's family had money, and that is why they thought Mom was a gold digger. Grams never really said. My mom was nineteen when I was born, and my dad was twenty-five.

"When I was ten, I wrote a letter to my dad's family. I sent a picture, thinking that they would at least want to see what their grandchild looked like. But they sent the picture back and said that I looked nothing like their son, and they did not want anything to do with me, and I wasn't to ever contact them again. My little heart was crushed from the rejection, and I cried himself to sleep for days."

"Was it hard knowing about your parents?" Amber asked. "Dying, that is?"

"Not really. How do you miss someone you haven't known? I called my grandmother 'Mom' once. She informed me that she was not my mother but my grandmother. So I started calling her Grams, and my granddad was Gramps."

"Why, didn't you go back to New York instead of coming to North Platte?"

Matthew explained that his grandparents had been up in age when they started to raise him. They hadn't had any children until Grams was in her forties. "That's when she got pregnant with my mom, so by time I came along, my grandparents were up in their late fifties or early sixties. I was eight when Gramps passed away. He was seventy-two at the time.

"Grams sold off the livestock and leased out the land to a neighboring farmer. Since Grams has passed away, there is nothing left for me to go back to.

"While I was in Vietnam," Matthew went on, "I met this guy who was originally from North Platte. His family had moved to Marysville, Kansas, when he was around eight. He talked about how great North Platte was, and when he got out of the service he was going to move back here. When I left the service with nowhere else to call home, I decided to come here and check it out for myself."

"Has the guy who was from here gotten out of the service yet?"

Mathew told her that Rick had died in a firefight less than three months after he arrived in Vietnam.

She looked at the time. "I need to get going! Didn't realize it was this late, I'll talk to you later."

Matthew wasn't sure if the news about Rick upset her or she really did have to go. Talking about Vietnam had brought back memories that he had tried to forget about.

The sun was starting to set in the west as he watched Amber walk away. When she stepped out from under the carport, the light of the setting sun caused her auburn hair to glisten and shimmer. He thought of how her hazel eyes seemed to sparkle and dance when she talked with him, as if she was so full of life and enthusiasm that she just had to let it out.

CHAPTER

8

The next time Amber came by, school was out for the summer vacation. She started talking as soon as she arrived.

"I wanted to get a summer job, but my dad told me not to," Amber said. "My mom and dad have a vacation planned. We are going back to Michigan to visit relatives. Since I will be graduating next year, and at that time I would need to go to work if I intended to go on to college."

After talking on for a while, she said, "I was wondering about the firefight you mentioned. Did very many die during that fight, and were you wounded? Did you ever have to shoot anyone?"

Matthew replied slowly, "I do not really like to talk about what happened in Vietnam. I still have nightmares off and on."

"I heard that it helps sometimes to talk about things," Amber said.

"I suppose you are right about that," he said. "There were about ten of us wounded, and only four were killed, which was amazing under the circumstances."

"Why was that?" she asked.

"We had just set up a base camp a few days earlier, and as far as we knew, we were the only ones in the area at that time. We had only been there a few days when the Viet Cong came out of the jungle, and they were as surprised to see us as we were to see them. We had no idea they were even in the area. We hadn't received any information about any Viet Cong in the area. I don't think they knew that we were there, either.

"We looked at them with a big question mark, like 'Where did you come from?' They stared back at us with a look that said, 'What are you doing here?' Then someone shouted, and the bullets started flying, along with some hasty mortar rounds. The commander called in an artillery strike.

"I was running from one individual to another. It was my job as a medic to try and keep as many people alive as possible. So when anyone hollered for a medic, I went. The firefight lasted for about thirty minutes. Once the artillery shells started dropping in, the Viet Cong faded back into the jungle.

"While I was doing what I could to patch up the wounded, the helicopters started arriving to remove those that were wounded along with those that had died. They were being airlifted back to base camp where the hospital was. I went to check on the other men in the unit.

"When the shooting started, I saw Rick headed for his assigned position, and I hollered at him to keep his head down. I found him later, not too far from where he was supposed to be.

Then someone said that I was bleeding, but I thought it was just blood that I had picked up from treating the wounded. They finally convinced me that it was indeed my own. I had been hit with shrapnel and didn't even know it. With so much confusion at the time and with the adrenalin running high, I hadn't felt anything.

"I was airlifted along with the other wounded

back to the base hospital, where they removed the shrapnel and patched me up. A few weeks later, four of us were sent back to the field.

"The first year I was there, not much went on. It had been an easy tour up to that point, so I decided to extend for another six months. With the combat pay and nothing to spend it on, I could save must of my paycheck, which went into a savings account. I was down to three and half months left on my extension when we got hit the first time. I had a month and a half left when we got hit the second time.

"This time a bullet grazed my right arm. I did not need someone to tell me I had been hit—it was like a hot poker when the bullet struck.

"They sent me back to base hospital, and after a few weeks they were talking about sending me back out to the field. Then no, they weren't. Then yes, they were. A doctor finally came in and gave me my marching papers to come back to the states.

"I was sent to Fort Hood, Texas, where I stayed until I was mustered out of the service. When I got out of the service I flew back to Fort Leonard Wood, Missouri, where I had my savings account. I closed out the account and came on to North Platte," he finished.

"You were a doctor then in the army?" Amber asked.

"No, dear, I don't have a medical degree. I was trained at the level of an EMT and was responsible for providing first aid and frontline trauma care on the battlefield. I was also responsible for providing continued medical care in the absence of a readily available physician. This included caring for any diseases and battle injuries, so they could be transported back to a hospital where the real doctors were. Though I could use a rifle, I did not carry one while performing my duties. I did carry a forty-five pistol, though I never used it."

CHAPTER

9

Amber looked a little uneasy about what Matthew had been telling her, and she changed the subject. "I am not looking forward to our trip to Michigan. We grew up out here, and I don't really know any of my cousins, aunts, uncles, and grandparents. They are mostly strangers to us girls.

"We have gone back to visit every so often, but not enough to feel like a part of the family tree back there. I know their mom and dad's folks, brothers and sisters. For me they are just people we visit from time to time. Besides, we are always going back to visit them, but they rarely come out here to see us. I don't remember any of them ever coming to Nebraska. We have always gone back there.

"Well, I best be getting home," she said abruptly. "Mom says there are things to do before we leave."

"Be positive, dear," Matthew said. "You may just have a good time even if they are strangers in a way."

"I will try to be positive," she said.

Amber was down to visit a few times before they left. The last time she was down was the night before they were to leave.

"Do you need any money in case you find something that you might want while you're gone?" Matthew asked.

"Oh Matthew, I couldn't take your money! How would I ever pay you back?"

"Well, honey, I wasn't expecting you to pay me back. How about forty dollars, just in case? You can't tell me you're a woman who wouldn't want a little spending money in her pocket. Besides, you might come across a dress, hat, shoes, or whatever else that might catch your fancy." He handed her a twenty, a ten, and two fives.

She looked at him, and then at the money.

"I don't have any family," he explained, "or anyone to share my money with except you. So please take it and find something nice for yourself. Besides, you have a birthday coming up in less than two weeks. Let's just consider this as an early birthday gift from me."

Amber hesitated but finally accepted the money. "I will bring you back something."

To which Mathew said, "Honey, all I ask is that you come back safe and sound, and do have a good time. You won't be gone forever, at least I hope not."

"Okay," she said. "You will still be here, won't you?"

"If the Lord is willing, I'll still be here. This place is just temporary, like I said before. But I am sure it will be a while before I have enough for a down payment on a permanent place."

CHAPTER

10

On the way to Michigan, Amber opened up about Matthew, telling her family things that she hadn't shared before. When her mother, Susan, had asked what the two of them talked about, Amber only mentioned the small stuff. Now she told them that after his folks had died when he was only three months old, he was raised by his grandparents and grew up on a farm in Upstate New York.

"He went into the service when he was eighteen," she went on, "and was sent to Vietnam as a field medic.

He's not a doctor. More like an EMT," an emergency medical technician.

"He patched up the wounded, so they could be transported to a base hospital. He was wounded twice." Amber also told them how and why he had come to be in North Platte instead of going back to New York.

John, her dad, said, "If he was wounded, he should have been given a Purple Heart."

"He didn't say anything about that," Amber said, "but I'll ask him next week when we get back home. He also gave me forty dollars. He said it was an early birthday gift in case I found something I might want while we're gone."

John and Susan looked at each other, and her mom said, "That sure was nice of him, dear."

"He told me he didn't have any family," Amber said, "and no one to share his money with except me."

Her dad looked at her mom. "Really?" John said. "What about his dad's family?"

"They don't want anything to do with him. He sent his dad's folks a letter with a picture of him when he was ten. They sent the picture back and said that he didn't look anything like their son and not to ever write to them again. His little heart was crushed. He said that he cried for days over it."

"How old is Matthew now?" Susan asked.

"He is twenty-one," Amber said.

"I wonder why he didn't continue to pursue the medical field," Susan said. "Especially after all that training that he had to get in order to be a medic in the first place."

"I would think that maybe he had had enough when he was in Vietnam," John said, "all that blood and gore he witnessed. I would imagine that he just wanted to get away from it. That would be my guess, anyway."

"Oh, by the way, Amber," her mom said, "we are not going right back home, dear. Your dad and I have saved up for this trip for quite some time. Since this will be the last year all of us will be able to spend time together as a family, with you graduating at the end of the school year, we are going to go sightseeing after we leave Michigan. We are going to be gone for at least a month. We wanted to spend time together as a complete family one last time this summer before you go off on your own."

Amber looked out the car window and said only, "Oh!"

While they were at her grandparents' house, a carnival set up downtown. Amber went with Ann and Angie to check it out. Later on they spent time out at the lake, swimming and fishing, taking boat rides and water skiing.

Amber didn't go swimming or skiing, but she did go for some boat rides, and she did some fishing. She moped about when they first got there, but after a while she came around. They were there for about a week altogether. She made friends with a few of her cousins but still felt more like a stranger. She was thinking that once she was on her own, she probably would never come back to visit.

The Saturday before they left, her mother and grandmother baked a cake and had an early birthday party for her. On a shopping trip over to Marshall, Amber bought herself a dress and a purse.

CHAPTER

11

Matthew went to work the day they left for Michigan. He kept hoping and praying that she would have a good time and the family would have a safe trip. The week went by rather quickly, and he was looking forward for her return. He enjoyed her company, even if she prattled on a lot. Amber had said her mother told her that she talked too much, and people would get tired of listening to her prattle all the time. But Matthew told her she could come by and prattle all she wanted. He found her quite delightful just the same.

Matthew was thinking they would be back by

the end of the next week at the latest. On Tuesday, July second, the day after Amber's birthday, a large and violent storm passed through the area with high winds, hail, and a torrential downpour. Matthew along with others spent the rest of the week cleaning up tree limbs, fixing damaged street signs, and unplugging storm drains.

At the end of the week, he received a postcard from Amber that had a picture of the Mackinac Bridge. The card read:

> Thought we would be home by now, came to Mackinaw city after we left the grandparents. We are going to upper Michigan, and then over into Wisconsin. I have been told that we will be gone for a MONTH.
>
> Amber

Matthew sat down and wrote a letter to Amber. He talked about the past week and all that was accomplished at work. He told her about the hailstorm, writing that he had gone down and checked their family's mobile home but didn't see any real damage.

The next week he received another postcard, which read:

We have seen Lake Superior, then on to Wisconsin Dell's. We're headed toward Deadwood South Dakota now, and we plan to see Mount Rushmore.

Amber

To the letter he had started about what had transpired at work, Matthew added that his neighbor, Sara, was always trying to find something negative about him so she could complain to Jackie about it. He would have the letter waiting for her when she returned home.

He found a spot to hang the postcards. Since Amber was the only one who ever come around and now was gone, he started to miss her even though he knew she was coming back. It was strange that he felt this way, considering that they had known each other only a few months, but for him it seemed like forever.

CHAPTER 12

At work, he was sent over to the park when the carousel quit working. Bud, his supervisor, was afraid that something serious might be wrong. It was old, and replacement parts were hard to find.

When Matthew arrived, the park employee said that he had to be somewhere else and would return later. He left Matthew a meter, some tools, and a locater for locating underground wires.

Matthew checked for electrical power at the breaker box going to the carousel itself, and following his train of thought, he checked at the fuse box below the light company's meter, where he found power. He disconnected the electrical power from its source, and having read the manual on how to use the locator, he hooked it up at the breaker box in the carousel. He followed the wires going back toward the meter. The first wire he checked was okay. About halfway between the carousel and the power pole is where he lost the signal on the second wire.

Retrieving a pick and shovel, he dug down to where the wire was and found that a gopher had chewed on it, causing the wire to short out and melt in two. The gopher did not survive the ordeal.

He left there and went over to an electrical store, where they told him how to make some simple repairs and supplied him with the necessary parts to do so. He was able to make the needed repairs with the parts. After hooking up the power source again, he turned the power back on and operated the carousel to ensure it was working okay. Then he filled the hole back in and picked up the tools.

As he was about to leave, the park employee and Bud the supervisor showed up. After they tried the carousel, they thanked him for fixing the problem.

After the repair in the park, he was asked to help Gary out with traffic lights once in a while. Gary was considered the foreman in the street department. There were two other guys besides him.

Several days after repairing the carousel, Matthew received another postcard, this time with a picture of Mount Rushmore:

> We have seen a lot of interesting places,
> I have been enjoying myself some, but I
> must say, I miss seeing you.
>
> Amber

Once again he added to the letter to keep her up to date on what had been going on while she was away. Yes, he was missing her, and he thought that maybe she was like a sister he never had.

The next post card to arrive was from Yellowstone and had Old Faithful on the front.

> We have seen buffalo, moose, bear,
> swans, and deer. Maybe I'll make it back
> someday, as nice as this is, I am anxious
> to get back home to my own bed.
>
> Amber

Matthew added more to the letter he was writing to her.

The family had now been gone for almost three

weeks when he got another postcard, this one came from the Grand Tetons.

> I think we are about ready to start home.
> I am so tired of riding, my butt hurts.
> Headed toward Laramie tomorrow.
> Hopefully home next.
>
> Amber

The postcard was dated four days ago, but there was still no sign of her.

CHAPTER

13

Matthew was sent back over to the city park, this time to the men's ball diamond to check out one of the scoreboards that was not working. He went up in the tower where the scorekeepers would be located to check the controller that operated the scoreboard.

First he tried the controller on another scoreboard, and it worked fine. Then he located the junction box where the cables from the tower and the scoreboard were connected. There he hooked up the controller to the cable going directly to the scoreboard itself.

After determining that the scoreboard was working okay, he left and picked up a new connector. After replacing the old connector coming from the tower, he went back upstairs and hooked the controller back up. After he tested the scoreboard's operation and everything was now working as intended, he informed his supervisor.

The weather was hot, as it has been for all of July. You didn't have to exert much energy, if any, to work up a sweat. By the end of the day, Matthew would be saturated in sweat. At home he almost needed a crowbar to pry his clothes off, as they were stuck to him like glue. Every day after work, the first place he headed was the shower.

It had been five days since the last postcard had been mailed. He was in the shower with the bathroom door open and had just finished washing his hair when he heard a much-missed voice out in the hall say loudly, "When are you going to get a couch and replace those ugly green towels?"

Matthew grinned, though she could not see it, and replied, "I am hurt that you do not appreciate my government-issued towels! Maybe you can go with me someday and pick out a sofa and some new towels. You have truly been missed, but I do hope you had a good time. If I wasn't in the shower, I would give you a big hug! I wrote you a letter, by the way. It is on the table with your name on it."

"I am glad to hear I was missed, and yes, in spite of everything I did have a good time. Just not at first. Seeing that I was already there, I decided that I might as well make the best of it. Did see a lot of interesting things, though, and I wouldn't mind going back to Yellowstone and the Grand Tetons someday.

"When we got to Laramie, Wyoming, Dad decided to take a run up through the Rocky Mountain National Park from a town called Granby. It took us over the mountain and into Estes Park, where we stayed for two days. It was an enjoyable ride and very scenic, but I just wanted to come home."

"Honey," Matthew said, "I need to get out now."

"Okay, I will go on out to the kitchen and wait for you."

After Matthew dressed, he went into the kitchen and gave her that big hug. She gave him a postcard from Estes Park and a vase that she had picked up in South Dakota. Then she proceeded to tell him all about their trip.

"I felt like a stranger, and out of place around my grandparents and the others, but then that is just what I am—a stranger. Angie kept telling everyone that I had a boyfriend. I did buy a few things for myself. Also for Ann and Angie."

"Honey, I haven't told you the whole story about my grandmother," Matthew said, "but I will if you have time, or it can wait."

"No, please tell me."

CHAPTER

14

My grandmother got sick when I was twelve, but she didn't tell me what was really wrong with her until just before she died. Grams had cancer, and she passed away just before my thirteenth birthday. I wanted to stay on the farm, but the powers that be wouldn't let me.

"They put me in a foster home, to start with. The foster people were not very nice, and they took it upon themselves to make my life miserable, especially their son and daughter. After a while I was taken to an orphanage several hundred miles away. No one wanted a teenager. They mostly wanted babies and younger children that they could mold into being a part of their own family and their way of life."

"Why an orphanage so far away?" Amber asked.

"I have thought about that. I believe that the authorities thought they could get rid of me, they would have free rein over the farm, and this way there was no one to interfere with their plans.

"Just before they took me to the orphanage, the foster parents had gone somewhere, and while they were gone, their son took it upon himself to try and be the boss. I had had enough of him, and I lost my temper and hit him. When the foster parents got back home, their son and daughter lied, saying I had hit him for no reason at all. The foster dad took a drop cord and beat me with it.

"I still have the scars from the beating, and I will as long as I live. I suppose that by taking me several hundred miles away, they also got rid of any evidence of what had happened to me."

"How could someone do that to you?" Amber asked, "Or anyone, for that matter. And you got nothing from the farm?"

"No, but I did have Grams Bible and some pictures, plus a locket that had belonged to my mother. They took me away in such a hurry that everything else got left behind. I was just a kid and never really understood what happened to the farm. I stayed in the orphanage until I turned eighteen. That is when I joined the army.

"The orphanage was run by nuns. Most of them were nice, but a few not so much. They tried to convert me into being a good Catholic, but I felt as if I would be letting Grams down if I did that. Grams was in church whenever the doors were open. We went to a Methodist church not far from the farm. To be truthful, I did not know where I stood with God at the time, and I suppose I still don't.

"Sometimes older kids would come to the orphanage, but they usually didn't stay long, as a relative would come by after getting court approval to take them in. All the kids who came to the orphanage were scared and felt abandoned, just the way I felt when I first arrived. These kids would either crawl into themselves or try to compensate by acting real tough and start pushing the other kids around. Some of the older kids would even run way."

After I had been at the orphanage for some time," Matthew continued, "it wasn't hard to read the new kids as to which way they would go. I interfered with the bullies and tried to help the ones that would crawl into themselves by putting up a wall. I wasn't always successful, but they knew I was there if they ever needed a friend or just wanted to talk.

"I left the orphanage before I finished high school. While I was stationed at Fort Hood, Texas, I obtained a GED, and I plan to take some night courses in electronics out at the college."

He thought for a moment, and Amber let the silence sit. "While you and your family were gone, we had a really bad storm go through, with damaging winds, hail, and a torrential downpour. It was on July second. I walked down and checked the outside of your mobile home but didn't see any damage. Don't know if your dad is aware of the storm that went through. He might want to check the roof, if he hasn't already."

"Okay, I will tell him. I best head back before they think I ran away."

Matthew thanked her for the vase. "It is really nice, and I will treasure it always. I enjoyed the postcards you sent. Did you have a nice birthday? And did you read your letter before I came from the shower?"

"No, I will read it later on." Amber showed him that she had it in her hand. "Mom and her mother baked me a cake, but there were no presents, which was okay. I think I am old enough to do without them, and besides you gave me forty dollars! I bought myself a dress and a purse for my birthday. I'll see you later, best be going."

"I am so glad you're back, dear." Matthew gave her another hug before she walked out the door.

CHAPTER

16

The next time she came to see him, she said, "I have been wanting to ask about something you told me when I was here before. I told dad about you being wounded while you were in Vietnam, and he thought you should have gotten a Purple Heart."

"I actually got two of them," Matthew said.

She said she would like to see them.

He went back to the bedroom and retrieved the box that he had had made with the Army logo on the top. It held all his personal information for the time when he was in the service. He brought it out to the table and opened it.

Matthew showed her his discharge papers, the certificate for his GED, and his birth certificate. Then he displayed the different ribbons he had gotten and told her what they stood for. He displayed his medals: two were Army Commendation Medals for meritorious service in the Republic of Vietnam, and one was an Army Commendation Medal that was a first oak leaf cluster for meritorious achievement. From the very bottom of the box, he took out two Purple Hearts and showed them to her.

Amber picked up each medal and curiously looked them over. As she held one of the Purple Hearts in her hand, she asked, "Where were you wounded?"

"Mostly on the front of my legs, and some on my torso, and of course my arm," he said, gesturing a little.

It took a couple of weeks for them to catch up on everything that happened during her trip and at home for him while she was gone.

One day, as Amber was heading up front to get the mail she walked by Matthew's place, and noticed that he had set out a gallon jug in order to make sun tea. She started laughing when she saw it. Later when she came to see him that evening, she said, "I noticed your jar of sun tea. It is going to be really strong and bitter."

"Why is that?" Matthew asked.

"Well, how many tea bags did you use?"

"The package said one tea bag per cup," he said, "so I figured up how many cups in a gallon, and I used that many tea bags."

She laughed. "That is if you're brewing one cup at a time. You only need three tea bags for sun tea, four at the most."

"Well, dear," he said, "if you haven't figured it out by now, when it comes to the kitchen, I am totally illiterate."

"Yes, I see your point. But I am sure you can learn to cook if you want to."

"I always thought that was a woman's job, I guess. On the farm I tended the animals, slopped the hogs, fed the chickens, cleaned out horse stalls, helped plant and harvest, and milked the cows. I even helped Grams clean the house a few times. But I was never taught how to cook."

"Well, if you are going to be a bachelor," Amber said, "you should at least have a cookbook and know a few basics besides peanut butter, baloney, and mayo sandwiches. Around here there are no hogs, chickens, or cows to feed, nor are there any fields to plant."

"I looked at a cookbook once," Matthew said, "but I didn't understand the language—one-half cup or two tablespoons really made no sense to me."

"Well, I am going to dump out the tea, and tomorrow you can try again. But only use three tea bags this time."

"Okay, dear, I will use only three tea bags."

The next morning, he sat out a jug of water with three tea bags in it. That night when she came down, they poured the tea over some ice cubes.

"I had better keep an eye on you from now on," Amber said. "If you want to make something and need any advice, just ask, okay?"

"Okay, I'll ask, and maybe you can help me figure out how to decipher a cookbook."

"Do you have one?" she asked.

"No I don't. Which one should I buy? I have noticed that there are several different ones."

"I'll pick you up one, okay?"

"Okay, but let me give you some money first."

"I still have money left over from my birthday."

"That is your money. I will give you some more for the cookbook."

Later that night, she talked to her folks about

going with Matthew to find a cookbook and get some better food than what he had been eating. So that Saturday, she went with him to pick up a cookbook, and later they went to the grocery store and picked up items that he had been avoiding. She explained to him how to read the ingredients list and measurements in the cookbook and how to cook some of the food they had purchased.

CHAPTER 17

Amber came down the night before school was to start. She said her mother had told her that if she needed to do any homework, she would have to do it before she went anywhere to visit.

Matthew agreed with her mother. "I wish I had been able to go to a regular school and get a better education." He supposed that while the problem was not entirely caused by going to the orphanage, at least half of it was. "I would offer to help you with any homework that you might have a problem with, but I am sure it would be beyond my ability to do so."

"That's okay," she said, "Maybe I can come down

and study here. There would be less interruptions here than at home. I will just have to convince mom there wouldn't be any distractions, though."

On Tuesday afternoon, Matthew went out to the community college and signed up for a night class in electronics. The class would be on Thursday evenings from seven to eight and would start right after Labor Day.

Before his schedule got busier with classes and cold weather set in, Matthew decided to get out and see more of the area for himself. He had heard some of the guys at work talking about a lake up by Ogallala, Nebraska, called Lake McConaughy and affectionately known as Big Mac.

The lake was formed when Kingsley Dam was built to hold back the waters of the North Platte River. Big Mac is twenty-two miles long and three and half miles wide at its greatest expanse. Matthew spent a Saturday afternoon at the lake before heading back home to North Platte. The fishing was great.

Matthew had heard about Sioux Lookout southeast of town and mentioned to Amber about wanting to go see it for himself. Amber said she would like to go with him. With her folks' approval, the two of them went to have a look on the second Saturday in September. Many people climbed to the top of the lookout, where there was a statue of an Indian, but Matthew and Amber decided not to take the time for a climb. From there they continued east to Fort McPherson National Cemetery just south of Maxwell, Nebraska, and then returned home.

Matthew had heard of many other sites—Ash Hollow State Historical Site, Chimney Rock National Historical Site, Courthouse and Jail Rocks, and Fort Robinson—but these would have to wait until spring.

CHAPTER

18

September went by fairly fast, it seemed. Matthew was kept busy with various projects along with helping with the traffic lights once in a while.

One day at the end of the month, when he came home and stopped to pick up his mail, he noticed a flyer on the bulletin board at the mail delivery room at the management office. The flyer, which had not been there the day before, was about a mobile home for sale in lot twenty-three. He took it with him and called the number listed when he got home, but there was no answer.

He left the flyer on the table and went back to take a shower. He was standing in front of the mirror with a towel around his waist when Amber came barging into the bathroom, all excited about finding the flyer about the mobile home. She asked if he was going to buy it.

Then she noticed the scars on his back that ran down to his legs. She walked over to him and ran her fingers across the scars. With tears in her eyes, she said, "I do not understand why someone would do this to another person."

Matthew said, "Honey, I really do care about you, but it is not a good idea for you to be in here right now."

She stepped back. "Are you going to buy this mobile home?" She held up the flyer, determined to get an answer before she left.

"I don't know, dear. We will need to look at the place first. I called the number that is listed but didn't get an answer."

She turned around to leave the room. "I think I know who owns this. I will call and see if anyone is home yet."

He was getting dressed in the bedroom when she came in excitedly. She said that the number put her in touch with someone named Linda, and they could meet her at seven that evening. The mobile home belonged to Linda's parents, Walt and Martha, who had moved in four years ago. About a year and half after that, Walt took sick and had trouble getting around. They had a deck built so he could go outside and sit without having to climb up and down the steps any more than necessary.

"Martha took care of him," Amber went on, "but it was quite stressful for her at times. Linda thinks that's the reason she ended up having a heart attack and dying. Walt couldn't stay by himself, and Linda has two kids to support, so she couldn't be around to take care of him. He is in need of constant care, so she had to place him in a living center for now, where he can get the care that he needs."

"Did she say how much they were asking?"

"No, I didn't think to ask her."

"Well then, if we are to be there by seven, I had best get something to eat before we go."

CHAPTER

19

After they ate, they drove down to lot twenty-three just before seven. Matthew noticed that the yard was a lot bigger than his was. The deck was pretty good-size, and there was room to park two vehicles. He got out and walked around to look the mobile home over. The mobile home was a Bonnevilla.

A car pulled into the driveway. A woman got out and asked if they were the McCrackens.

Amber said, "Yes, we are."

Matthew looked at Amber with raised eyebrows and a smile. Amber smiled back.

Linda introduced herself. She explained that when her dad got ill, her folks deeded the mobile home over to her. It was just a two-bedroom, and with a daughter and a son, she needed three bedrooms. She would use the money to help pay for her dad's care center.

Linda unlocked the door, and they stepped into a living room. To their right was a short hallway that led into the kitchen. There was a front dining area with a built in desk on one side next to some cabinets. The kitchen counters were in a horseshoe shape with a lot of cupboard and counter space.

Matthew commented that he didn't know much about getting around in a kitchen, but he thought this one was really nice.

Amber agreed. They went on through the trailer toward the back. The first room they came to was a bedroom. Next was a laundry area by the back door, and then a bathroom, with a bedroom in the very back of the trailer. The hallway was on the opposite side of the trailer compared to the one he was in now.

After talking about the features of the mobile home, they went back into the kitchen. Matthew looked around a bit more and said, "I am impressed with this kitchen, and the built in desk is really nice also."

He asked Linda how much she was asking. She told him that she wanted to get at least $8,500 for it.

He thought about it for a while and then asked about the utilities. She showed him the previous bills for gas and electricity. He asked about water, sewer, and anything else he would need to know about.

"The water and sewer are included in the lot rent," Linda said.

Then Matthew said, "I don't suppose you would take a bank draft, would you?"

She laughed. "Yes, I will."

Matthew said that he would need to go to the bank, as the money was in his savings account. He would get a bank draft for the amount, and then he could meet up with her at the courthouse and do the transaction there, if that is where they needed to go.

Linda said that she could meet him the next day around two, if that would work for him. He agreed to the time.

Amber and Matthew left. He dropped Amber off at home, and she was telling her folks about the mobile home before she had even closed the door.

CHAPTER

20

The next day Matthew asked Bud if he could have the afternoon off and explained why. Bud said he could and congratulated him on his new home—if Matthew was willing to buy a home, then more than likely he was going to be staying there permanently.

At noon he went over to the bank and picked up a bank draft for the amount of the mobile home. He then stopped by a moving company, picked up some boxes, and rented an appliances hand truck for moving appliances. He was sitting outside the courthouse at two when Linda arrived.

He got up and met her on the sidewalk leading up to the courthouse. Inside they talked to one of the clerks about transferring the deed to his name. Then he gave Linda the check for the $8,500.

Linda said, "I am still going through my mom and dad's belongings. I plan to have a yard sale in a couple weeks, if you would be interested."

After Matthew left the courthouse, he went by the phone company to have his phone service moved and then to the gas and power companies to have the bills changed over to his name.

On the way back to his rental he stopped to tell Jackie that he would be moving over to lot twenty-three because he had bought the mobile home there. He said that he would try to be out of the rental before the first of November.

Later Amber came down, still very excited about him buying the mobile home. "Now I don't have to worry that you are going to move away and I will never see you again!" She looked at the deed to the trailer. "It is really yours? When are you going to move?"

"I told Jackie that I would try to be out of here by the first of November. Which only gives me six days."

He started putting boxes together, and Amber started filling them in the kitchen. Then Matthew went to the bedroom, and started filling boxes as he cleaned out the drawers.

Around six thirty, Amber's parents and sisters stopped by on their way to Wednesday night church service and invited him to go along. Matthew had seen Amber's folks from a distance but this was the first time actually meeting them. Matthew agreed to go and said he would follow them.

It had been a while since Matthew had been to church. He had felt like something was missing in his life, and just maybe this was it.

"Would it be okay if I ride with Matthew?" Amber asked.

At the car, Matthew opened the door for her to get in and walked around to open it for her again when they arrived at the church.

The six of them walked into the church together. He was introduced to the pastor and several others. He sat next to Amber with the rest of her family. When they stood up to sing the first hymn, he held the hymnal with one hand, and without thinking about it he put his arm around Amber as they shared the hymnal.

After the service was over and they were walking out to the cars, John asked, "Did you enjoy the service?"

"Very much so," Matthew replied. "I haven't gone to church since my grandmother passed away. Well, except for the time I was in the orphanage. It was mandatory that we attend Mass. I had trouble with the Catholic services, as I did not always understand what was being said. It has been way too long. I am sure that Grams will be happy to see me back in church again."

"Well then, Matthew, you will have to keep coming."

"Okay, Mr. Marshall, I will do that."

"When do you plan to get moved?" John asked.

"I was hoping to be completely moved by Saturday. I will need to clean once I am out of the rental."

"If you need any help, just let us know," John said.

"Thank you for the offer. I will keep that in mind, and I believe Amber wants to go and find a sofa. She seems to think I need one."

"It's time to go, you two," Amber's mom called out from the car.

Matthew drove Amber home and walked her up to the door, wishing her a good night. "I will see you tomorrow, then," he said.

Amber looked disappointed that he hadn't kissed her. *Should I have kissed her?* Matthew found himself thinking as he headed for home. *I am not too sure about that yet. Would her dad even approve of such a bold move on my part?*

Back at the rental, he continued to fill and label boxes. He loaded them into the back of the station wagon and drove down to the mobile home he had bought. He carried the boxes in and put them in the room where they would need to be unpacked. Back at the rental, he loaded up the recliner, the end table, and a few other items, and took them over to his new home. It was after midnight before he called it quits.

CHAPTER

21

When Matthew got home on Thursday, he stripped the bed, took it apart, and put it in the car along with the nightstand, the kitchen table, and the two chairs. By the time he was finished loading them into the car, Amber had showed up, and she rode down with him to the mobile home.

As soon as they got there, Amber started cleaning the cabinets and counters before putting anything away.

While Amber was working on the kitchen, Matthew carried the twin bed to the spare bedroom and brought in the other furniture from this load. Then he went back down to the rental and collected the clothes from the closet. He filled a box with items from the bathroom, and another box with everything from the fridge.

When he arrived with the next load, Amber's two younger sisters were there, trying to help unload boxes but they were just mostly underfoot. He took the box of items from the fridge into the kitchen and then the clothes to the back bedroom, where he hung them up. He made up the bed in the spare bedroom, as he intended to sleep there that night.

Amber's dad came down a while later and went down to the rental with Matthew. They gathered up any items that were still there to be moved. John helped load the washer into the back of the station wagon, which meant leaving the tailgate down. After they strapped everything down, they took the washer to his new trailer, unloaded it, and took it inside. Then they went back down for the dryer.

Once the washer and dryer were in place, John asked Matthew if he had brought the tools they needed.

"Yes, I left them in the back of the car. I will go and get them."

"All right," John said, "I will start hooking up the hoses."

Once the dryer was connected, John and Matthew went back for the stereo.

By this time Amber and her mother had cleaned the kitchen and put stuff away. After John and Matthew delivered the stereo system along with some other items, it had gotten late, so everyone went home.

CHAPTER

22

When Matthew got off work on Friday, he swung by a fast food restaurant and picked up something to eat, then went back to his new home. Amber showed up a while later, and they started putting things away in the bathroom and the bedroom.

When Amber's family arrived, John and Matthew went back to the rental and picked up the lawn mower, garden hose, and the sprinkler, along with the lawn chair and the small table.

On the way back to the trailer, Matthew said, "I will need to go and get another bed now that I have a permanent residence. I also know Amber has something in mind for a sofa. She has been after me about not having one."

After everything was unloaded and put away, Matthew said he would go down and get the rental cleaned in the hope of giving the keys back the next morning.

"And after you return the keys," Amber said, "we will go and get a sofa, yes?"

"Okay, dear, we will go and get a sofa, if your folks are okay with you going along."

"I don't know," Susan said. "What do you think, dear?"

"If we don't let her go, she will be hard to live with," John said.

"I suppose you're right," Susan said. "Okay, then she can go." Then she and John laughed.

They all went down to the rental, and everyone pitched in. With all the help, it did not take long to clean it from one end to the other, and to investigate all the closets, nooks, and crannies for anything that might have been missed during the moving.

CHAPTER 23

Saturday morning, as Matthew was drinking a cup of coffee, Amber came knocking on the door. He let her in, then said, "I suppose with the weather turning cold, you would probably like a key, so you won't have to wait for me to open the door."

"That would be nice," Amber said with excitement.

He asked what she was doing up so early. "The stores don't open for some time yet."

"I found the perfect couch, and it is on sale!" She laid a flyer from the newspaper in front of him, showing a sectional couch that reclined on one end, with a twin-size hide-a-bed on the other end.

"I didn't know if this will fit in the living room," he said.

Amber thought it would, but suggested, "We can measure the spot where it is to go and see if there is enough room for it when we measure the couch at the furniture store. A bigger kitchen table with six chairs would be nice too."

They left a few hours later and dropped off the keys at the office. Jackie returned his deposit, and he paid for the next month's lot rent.

From there they went to Whitaker's Furniture. A salesman came over and asked if he could help them.

Amber showed him the flyer from the paper. "Do you still have this sectional?"

The salesman took them over to three sectionals in different colors.

Amber chose the blue one. Matthew sat down on the recliner and put his feet up. Amber sat down beside him and put her feet up next to his. "This is cozy," she said. Matthew looked at her and smiled.

They checked out the hide-a-bed and then measured to see whether the couch would fit. They determined that it would, and before Matthew could say anything, Amber said, "We will take it."

Then they looked at the kitchen tables until they both found one they liked, but Matthew didn't care for the chairs. The salesman said that they could choose a different set of chairs, so together they found a set of six chairs that they both liked.

Then they looked at double and queen-size beds. They chose the queen with matching nightstands. He could have paid for the furniture in cash, but it would have left him with not much in the bank. He opted to put down half and pay the rest in six-month installments. Whitaker's was to deliver the furniture that afternoon.

From there they went by Sears and picked up bedding for the new bed, then over to Hinky Dinky's groceries and back to the trailer. He stored the recliner he had already in the spare bedroom, along with the kitchen table and two chairs.

Amber started washing the new sheets and bedding. Later that afternoon the furniture had arrived. They brought the bed in first, then the nightstands, the four parts of the sectional, and last the table and six chairs. After the men from Whitaker's left, Matthew sat down at the table with a cup of coffee and some cookies they had just bought.

He sat there for a while not saying anything. Amber finally said, "A penny for your thoughts."

CHAPTER

24

Finally, Matthew spoke. "Honey, I kind of thought of you as a sister that I never had, but I have since changed my mind. You have been good for me, and I just hope that I have also been good for you."

She smiled from ear to ear. "Oh honey, I am sure you are good for me, and I would rather not be your sister, if it's all the same to you."

Her folks came down with a housewarming gift. John tried out the sofa and asked what Matthew was going to do with the recliner and the kitchen table and two chairs.

"I didn't know," Matthew said. He asked if John wanted the recliner.

"No," John said, "but there is a couple at church who are just starting out, and they don't have much in the way of furniture yet. I am sure that they could use the recliner, and the table and chairs, if that would be okay with you?"

Matthew said that it would be fine with him, so John made a phone call. After he talked with the couple a moment, John and Matthew loaded everything into the back of the station wagon to take over to them.

"We will stop on the way back and pick up something for supper," John said.

"We have supper already in hand," Susan said, "so don't be gone too long."

Matthew and John loaded up the table and chairs, and Matthew drove over to a small apartment. The couple was grateful for the furniture.

"We don't have much money, but we could pay a little every week," the husband said, "if that's okay."

"Who said anything about money? You can have it just to get it out of my way," Matthew said with a smile. "Well, Dad," he continued, "Mom said to get right back, so we best be going."

While John and Matthew were gone, Susan started asking Amber questions. She wanted to draw Amber out as to whether anything had gone on romantically between her and Matthew.

Amber got very serious. "I know he likes me, a lot even, and he puts his arm around me at church, which I really do like. It makes me feel like I am really his, but Mom, he hasn't once tried to kiss me. He told me earlier that he had thought of me as a sister he never had but now has changed his mind. He said that I was good for him, and he hoped that he was good for me."

"What did you say?" Susan asked.

"I told him that I was sure he was good for me, and I didn't want to be his sister, if that was okay with him. What if he asks me to marry him? Do you think I can say yes, or would Dad be against it?"

Susan shrugged. "You will have to wait and see on that one."

They had the table already set when Matthew and John returned.

"I guess Ann and Angie will have to sit at the breakfast bar and eat off paper plates," Susan said.

"We will need another set of dishes to make a service for eight," Amber said, "so no one will have to eat off paper plates."

"*We?*" her mom asked, and Ann and Angie laughed.

The adults sat at the table. John brought up about the farm. He asked Matthew if he had ever thought about going back to New York and maybe getting some justice for the farm.

"I haven't really thought about it," Matthew said. "I just figured it was gone, and I am sure that whatever transpired was done legally through the court. I might just stir up a hornet's nest if I went back. I've always thought I would be better off if I just left it alone. I haven't heard from anyone back there since they ran me out of town, more or less, and I am content with my life as it is."

CHAPTER

25

Later on that night as John and Susan lay in bed, John said, "Matthew called me Dad when we were getting ready to leave the Wilsons' apartment."

"Amber told me that Matthew had said she was good for him, and he hoped that he was good for her," Susan said. "She also wanted to know what to do if he asked her to marry him. I said she would have to wait and see. I really do like him, and I know you do too."

"Yes," John said, "he would make a good son-in-law, and I am sure that he loves her. I just don't think that he has totally realized it yet."

On Sunday, Matthew returned to church with Amber and her family. The minister talked about the fact that all have sinned and come short of the glory of God, as it is said in Romans 3:23; that there is none righteous, no not one, as in Romans 3:10; that John 3:16–17 says God so loved the world that he gave his only begotten Son, that whosoever believes in him should not perish but have everlasting life. God sent his Son into the world not to condemn the world, the pastor said, but so that the world through him might be saved.

Then he quoted 2 Peter 3:9: "The Lord is not slack concerning his promise, as some men count slackness; but is long-suffering to us-ward, not willing that any should perish, but that all should come to repentance."

Matthew remembered things his grandmother had said that he had not fully understood the meaning of at the time. The way the pastor talked about scripture was starting to make some sense to him, or maybe after all this time he was just ready to hear what was being said.

CHAPTER

26

Monday was filled with a lot of work to do, and Matthew hadn't stopped to think much about what the minister had said the day before. When he got home, Amber was there waiting.

"Hi, honey. This is a surprise. I thought you had to have your homework completed before you went to visit."

"I don't have any homework, and I am fixing supper. I am also making a list of items that I thought we could use. I know you have spent quite a lot of money already, and we don't have to buy all of these items at once. Another set of dishes would be top on the list, so when everyone comes down to eat the girls won't have to use paper plates.

"I was also thinking that we could have an open house one of these days. Invite people from church to come over for coffee and maybe some finger food, chips and dips, cookies, and some cake. It will give them a chance to get to know you, and you to know them."

"I see," Matthew said with a hint of playfulness. "Am I to suppose that you want me to make the finger food, cookies, and cake?"

Amanda laughed. "No! Mom and I will prepare everything. We have already talked it over, and mom thought it would be a nice gesture to invite people from church, and those who would like to come by can do so." She hesitated. "If you don't mind, Mom also suggested you might want to get a suit for church."

"Okay," Matthew said.

"How about this Saturday," she asked, "to go and see what we can find?"

"Honey, you do remember what Linda said, that she was going to have a yard sale this coming Saturday? I was thinking about going there to take a look-see, if that would be okay with you. We could go early in the morning and be back by ten, depending on what time she plans to start."

"Okay, I still have her number. I will give her a call."

After Amber hung up the phone, she said, "Linda said she was starting at eight on Saturday. I'll come down around seven, and we can go there first. When we return home, I'll call Mom and let her know that we're back." Amber laughed. "In case you haven't noticed, Mom and Dad like you. Dad said, 'I hope he knows what he has got himself into!'"

Wednesday at church, the minister spoke further on forgiveness and salvation from Romans 10:9–10, how if we confess Jesus as Lord and believe in our hearts that God has raised him from the grave, we will be saved, for we believe with the heart to find righteousness, and we confess with the mouth to seek salvation.

Matthew considered all that was said for some time as he lay in bed that night. He knew without question that he fit into the sinner category. Yet he was still fuzzy on exactly what to do about it. What was suggested seemed too easy. There must be something else that he should be doing.

CHAPTER 27

Saturday morning, Amber showed up before Matthew had even got out of bed. After calling out to make sure that Matthew was decent, she came into the bedroom. Once she was sure he was fully awake, she went back out to the kitchen and made coffee while he was getting ready. After breakfast, they left and arrived at Linda's shortly after eight.

Linda greeted them and told them to look around. "People started showing up by seven thirty," she said, "before I could even get everything put out."

Matthew noticed the outdoor table with the two

chairs. He was sure it would have been out on the deck at the trailer and went to look them over while Amber was browsing the tables filled with household items for sale. "How much for the table and chairs?" he asked Linda.

Linda gave him a price, and Matthew said that he would take them. Then he went to look at a corner curio cabinet that Linda had on display. He asked what she was asking for it, and after she had told him, he said that he would take that too.

Amber found a twelve-piece set of dishes still in the original boxes and some knickknacks for the curio cabinet. By time they left, they had the back end and the top of the wagon fully loaded. Amber's mom and dad were already there when they got back to the mobile home.

While Matthew and John carried items inside, Amber told her mom about the dishes and everything else they had bought. "Linda told me that her mom bought the dishes with the idea that the whole family would get together and use them, but that never did happen, so they were still in the box."

"We won't let that happen," Susan said.

Matthew put the curio cabinet in the corner, but it leaned forward and would not sit back against the wall as it should. John showed him what the problem was. After pulling the corner of the carpet back out of the way, John removed the corner portion of the slats that held the carpet in place and were keeping the curio cabinet unleveled. After John put the carpet back in place, the cabinet leveled out and set against the wall as it was supposed to.

Meanwhile, Amber had polished the curio cabinet, and when it was put back in place, she arranged the knickknacks in it.

They left the house and stopped at Roger's Café on the south end of town for dinner. Afterwards they moved on to Hirschfield's, a men's clothing store where Susan had him try on several different suits.

"Matthew, young man," John said, "you don't know what you have gotten yourself into."

Finally, after he had tried on several different suits, everyone was in agreement on a light-blue western-cut suit. It would need some tailoring yet.

Matthew paid for the suit and bought some dress slacks and a dress shirt for the time being. From there they went to the Bible supply store, where he picked up a study Bible, a Bible dictionary, and a copy of Strong's Concordance, along with several Christian novels to read for pleasure.

CHAPTER

28

Sunday's sermon from the book of Daniel was both interesting and very enlightening. By afternoon he was down at the Marshalls' home, having dinner.

John was a football fan, especially when it came to the Huskers, the Denver Broncos, or the Lions. Matthew hadn't had much to do with sports out on the farm or at the orphanage, so John was trying to explain what was going on, or at least trying to educate him on the subject.

Sunday night's topic was reading and studying the Bible. Matthew learned from 2 Timothy 2:15–16 to study to show yourself "approved unto God, a workman that needeth not to be ashamed, rightly dividing the word of truth. But shun profane and vain babblings: for they will increase unto more ungodliness."

In 2 Timothy 3:16–17, it is said that "all scripture is given by inspiration of God, and is profitable for doctrine, for reproof, for correction, for instruction in righteousness: That the man of God may be perfect, thoroughly furnished unto all good works."

That the man of God caught Matthew's attention. Did that include him? Could he be a man of God? Doubt was starting to float around in the back of his mind.

One day the next week, Matthew was sitting in the living room, reading the Bible, while Amber was doing her homework at the kitchen table. There was a knock at the door. When Matthew answered, a man introduced himself.

"I am Joseph Reed. I am a private investigator and was asked to talk with you, if that would be okay."

Matthew let him in, and they went into the kitchen for coffee. The private investigator said that he had been hired by the firm of Baskins & Martin, Attorneys-at-Law, to locate a Matthew McCracken.

"I just need to verify that you are the right

Matthew McCracken that they have been looking for. If you don't mind, I would like to ask you some questions."

"Yes, that would be okay, I guess," Matthew said.

Amber had put her homework aside and was listening with keen interest.

"What were your mom and dad's names?"

"June and Bob McCracken."

"And your grandparents' names?"

"Ted and Mary Rivers."

"Your birth date?"

"Tenth of February, 1947. What exactly is this all about, anyway?" Matthew asked.

"All I know is what I have been asked to do. Do you have a birth certificate I could use to verify this information?"

Matthew went back to the bedroom and brought out the box that contained all his personal records, from which he pulled out his birth certificate and handed it over.

Suddenly everything that had happened to him after his grandmother died swept over him like a giant wave.

"I don't understand why you or the law firm would need this information," he said heatedly. "After my grandmother died, I was taken off the farm, and put in a foster home, where I was beaten with a drop cord." He removed his shirt and T-shirt showing the private investigator his scarred back.

Amber added quietly, "It goes down his back, and the back of his legs ... and I assume across his buttocks."

"They left me laying on the floor while everyone else went to bed. I got up around three thirty in the morning, and fighting through the pain I left the house and walked to the hospital through the snow to seek medical attention. When the police arrived, they took pictures of my injuries, and the next day I was put in the back of a car and taken several hundred miles away to an orphanage, where I stayed until I turned eighteen.

"I just figured that they needed to get me out of town to cover up what had been done to me. And with me out of the way, the law could take possession of my grandparents' farm and reap the benefits from it."

"I don't know anything about that," the investigator said. "I was just hired to locate you and send my findings back to Baskins & Martins. I am sure that they will be contacting you and will explain everything. I am sorry for what happened to you. Have a nice night." And he left.

"That was strange," Amber said. "It must have

something to do with the farm, or what happened to you. When I go home, I would like to tell my mom and dad about the private investigator showing up. What do you think will happen next?"

"I guess we will have to wait to find out," Matthew said. Then he apologized to Amber for his sudden tirade. "I just felt so frustrated over the farm and everything that happened to me after Grams died. I remember the lawyers being there when they took me off the farm. The truth is, I did not go willingly.

"But while Joseph was still talking and I had given him the information he was asking for, I realized that if everything that happened to me had not happened, I would more than likely not even be here. Which means I would have never met you. Once again, dear, I apologize for my behavior earlier."

"It is okay, Matthew. I understand."

CHAPTER

29

A few days later, Matthew was about to leave the house for work when the phone rang. When he answered, it was his supervisor. Bud asked him not leave, as he would be by to pick him up.

"I will be waiting then," Matthew said.

When Bud arrived, Matthew went out and got in his car. "What's up?"

"Gary came by last night," Bud said, "and dropped off his keys along with the pager. He said he was leaving town and was not coming back. I think he is headed for California. I know he has mentioned it several times. I have heard that you are taking an electronics course out at the college."

"Yes, I started right after Labor Day," Matthew said.

"Well, since you have worked with Gary on traffic lights, I have decided to move you into his job. I picked you up this morning because you will be getting the work truck and the pager. You will be on call twenty-four hours a day, and you can take the truck home in case you get called out at night. Once we are back at the office, I will update the police dispatchers that you will be doing traffic lights now."

It was a lot to take in at once, but when they were in the office, Matthew got the pager and the keys for the truck from Bud, and started looking into the traffic lights. He wanted to read anything and everything that he could find on the subject. The rest of his day was spent going over what he already knew and what he could glean from the material he found.

That night when he arrived home, Amber was there, looking worried. "The car was here, but you were not. I was afraid something had happened to you."

Matthew explained that his supervisor had picked him up that morning, and he was now the official traffic light repairman along with his other tasks. He would be driving the work truck home from now on in case he got called out at night. He would be carrying a pager and was on call twenty-four seven.

CHAPTER 30

Several weeks later, Amber and Matthew were eating supper at the table when the phone rang. Amber answered it. "Yes, he's here." She handed Matthew the phone, saying, "It's that law firm."

Matthew spoke into the phone. "This is Matthew."

The woman on the other end said, "Matthew, I am calling from Baskins & Martins, the firm your grandmother hired to handle her estate. The private investigator who spoke with you recently has filled us in on some very disturbing news. When we went to the courthouse and searched the records, we found the report on the whipping and have viewed the photographs that were taken of the incident. We are looking into it, but as far as we can tell, nothing was ever done about it. Unfortunately, so much time has passed that we doubt there is much that *can* be done now.

"At the time, we thought you were in foster care and had no idea that you had been taken to an orphanage. Once we discovered what had happened, we started looking for you, but by time we located the orphanage you were taken to, you were already gone. We discovered that you had joined the military, so we were waiting for you to get out. When you got out, we thought you would come back to your hometown. Now we understand why you didn't, but you eluded us until we could track you down again.

"We have some things that we have kept for you, and we will be sending them your way. Of course, you will need to sign for them, but that should not be a problem. It will ensure that you have received everything that was bequeathed to you by your grandparents. Please accept our apology, for we had no idea what had transpired at the foster home."

"I appreciate that you have looked after Grams estate," Matthew said. "I am sorry if I have gotten the wrong idea about what happened to it."

"Under the circumstances, we can understand why you would think the way you did. The farm has been liquidated, and you will be receiving a check for the sale of it. If you have any questions, please give us a call, and if there is anything that we might find out further in reference to what happened at the foster home, we will let you know. I do not think we would need you to testify, as we have the pictures as evidence. Thank you for your time."

After he hung up, Amber said, "Then you are going to get some kind of an inheritance."

"It seems so. We will just have to wait until the items arrive to know just what it will be, though."

CHAPTER
31

Two days before Thanksgiving, Matthew received a notice from the post office that he had three packages to pick up. The next day he went to the post office and gave the slip of paper to the postal clerk. The clerk brought out the three packages. One box was fairly long, and another was smaller but of good size. The last package was a large envelope. He put the boxes in the back of the truck and headed for home.

At the trailer, he unloaded the boxes and put them in the living room. Then he opened the envelope. The letter pretty much said what the woman from

Baskins & Martins had already told him on the phone. There were also two checks in the envelope, one for $97,763.23, and the other for $23,972. The letter indicated that the larger check was for the sale of the farm and its remaining assets, less lawyer fees. The smaller check was from a life insurance policy and what had been in a savings account, plus interest and less his grandmother's funeral costs. Inside this larger envelope was another envelope with his name on it, containing pictures of his backside taken by the police when he was in the hospital.

Matthew put the larger envelope in a desk drawer in the kitchen along with the pictures, and then drove over to the bank, where he deposited both checks into his savings account. After the standard waiting time for the checks to clear, he would transfer some money into his checking account.

When he got home after work that day, Amber was there waiting for him. She was excited about the boxes she had discovered in the living room and was rather anxious to see what was inside them.

"I am going to take a shower," Matthew said, "and we will tackle the boxes after we have eaten."

Amber was disappointed. She thought Matthew would be more anxious to see what was in the boxes than he seemed to be.

After his shower, they sat down to eat. "I know you're anxious to see what is in the boxes," Matthew said. "I am too, but it has been eight years now, and I am sure a few more minutes will not hurt anything."

When he finally opened the smaller of the two boxes, they found four small boxes inside, each one labeled with its contents. He opened the first box and removed a pair of porcelain turtledoves, commenting that he had admired them as long as he could remember. Amber put them in the curio cabinet.

The other boxes contained a crystal butterfly, a pair of figurines of a boy and a girl kissing, and a teddy bear with a red heart on its chest. Amber also put those in the curio cabinet.

At the bottom of this same box were two photo albums that Matthew thought he would never see again. They contained photos of his mom and dad and of his grandmother and grandfather, along with his baby pictures.

There were three albums of classical music that he had grown up with, and a tarnished tin box full of old coins, some dating back to the late 1800s, along with around sixty dollars in two-dollar bills. He also found Grams Bible, his mother's locket, and some photos of his grandparents along with his mom and dad that had been left behind at the foster home.

Matthew had thought he would never see these things again.

In the bigger box were items that had belonged to his granddad: pocket watch, a pocketknife, a .30-06 lever action rifle, a .45 caliber pistol with holster and ammo belt, a pair of binoculars, an army canteen with a web belt, and several other items. Matthew put the rifle in the closet, and the pistol in the bottom drawer of the built-in dresser in his bedroom. The canteen and binoculars he put on the self in the closet.

"We will need to get a safe," he said, "for the coins and two-dollar bills, and the box that has all my personal records in it."

The two of them sat down and looked through the photo albums together. There were pictures of him growing up on the farm, feeding the chickens and sitting on a tractor when he was about four years old. Tears came to his eyes as he revisited times gone by, and he was overjoyed with what he had received. He was glad that there were still some honest people in the world. The lawyers could have kept it all to themselves, and no one would have been any wiser.

After they had everything put away, he knocked down the boxes so they could be taken to the trash in the morning. Then he showed Amber the letter from the law firm and told her about the money.

"I suppose now that you have that much money," Amber said, "you will want to buy a house."

"No, honey," Matthew said, "this will do fine. At least until we outgrow it."

Until we outgrow it did not escape her attention, but Amber didn't say anything. When she got home, she said, she would relate what had arrived in the two boxes, but would leave out the part about the money for now.

After she left, Matthew sat down and wrote a letter of appreciation to the lawyers, thanking them for their honesty.

CHAPTER

32

As Thanksgiving got closer, more forecasts of snow in the area were coming in. Matthew had been invited to the Marshalls' home for Thanksgiving dinner. The day before, a light snow had started to fall just after noon and was still falling when he walked Amber home later that night. By the time he went to bed, the snow had become much heavier.

The phone rang around twelve thirty on Thursday morning. It was his supervisor, Bud. "Because of the holiday, we are short of people, and we're in need of help plowing snow."

"I will come in and help," Matthew said. He left a note for Amber, saying that he had been called in to help plow snow and didn't know when he would get back home. He wished her and her family a blessed Thanksgiving, then he left for work.

They put him in a truck and gave him a list of streets to plow. As the morning was starting to get brighter, he had about half of the list completed, but with the snow still coming down, along with the high wind, what he had already done was covered over again. When he returned to the shop to fuel up around two thirty that afternoon, Bud told him to go home. By the time he arrived back at the trailer, it was close to three thirty.

Amber was there waiting for him. She said that she had been worried and felt bad that he had missed out on Thanksgiving dinner. "But I have brought some leftovers down, and I will get them heated up for you."

Matthew took off his insulated coveralls and overboots, and went to take a shower. While he was in the shower, Amber came in with a cup of coffee to ask how it had gone.

"They are short of help because of the holiday," Matthew said. "You get several roads cleared, and the first one you had done is already covered over again.

We are doing mostly the main roads and snow routes, and going ahead of emergency vehicles so they can get to where they need to go. I will more than likely be out again in the morning sometime. I will leave you another note if they call me."

After the shower, he came back out to the kitchen and ate the leftovers she had brought.

"I was really disappointed that you weren't there for thanksgiving," Amber said. "Dad said, 'When you have a job that supports you, you sometimes have to work when it isn't convenient.' He was sure that you would have rather been with us than working."

"Yes, I was really looking forward to having Thanksgiving dinner with you and your family. I was hoping I would be able to watch some football with Dad. It would have been great to have had a home-cooked Thanksgiving meal for a change.

"Sometimes there are things that interfere with our plans, but that is the way life goes, and complaining won't change anything."

CHAPTER 33

When Amber came home, her mother remarked, "You're back early."

"Matthew went to bed. He said there's a good chance that he will get called back out again tonight, as they are short of people due to the holiday weekend." A thought popped into her head. "If he had gotten the money before he bought the mobile home, I suppose he would have bought a house instead, and I wouldn't have ever seen him again."

"What money?" Susan asked.

"Oh—" It was too late to take it back, but she

didn't know whether she should've shared this. "It was part of his inheritance."

"You mean besides all the stuff in the boxes, he got some money also?"

"Yes, around one hundred and thirty thousand. He put it in the bank." Now she was afraid he would be upset with her because she had said something about it.

"He will have to pay an inheritance tax," John said. "The IRS and the state will take, at best, ten percent or more."

"After all he has gone through?" Amber said. "That's not fair."

"Fair or not," John said, "the Bible says to give to Caesar what is Caesar's, and to God what is God's. In other words, we are to pay taxes, for in this case 'Caesar' is the IRS and the state.

"I've been wondering," he continued, "do you think Matthew is a Christian?"

"He has never said he was. He does read the Bible, and he doesn't drink alcohol. He doesn't smoke, and I've never heard him use profanity."

"Well, honey, after being in the army it is amazing he doesn't do any of those things," John said.

"I think his grandmother had a lot of influence

on him growing up," Amber said. "I know she is the reason he won't drink."

"Not doing those things is all well and good," John said, "but it doesn't make him a Christian, nor does going to church."

"He seems interested in what the minister has to say, and he is asking questions," her mom said. "So I believe he is at least searching for the right answers."

"With all that he has gone through," John said, "you might have thought he would give up on God."

"Maybe it has drawn him closer to God," Susan said.

CHAPTER

34

Around two thirty the next morning, Matthew was called back in to work. He left a note on the table just before he left, and was put to work plowing as soon as he got there. With the wind as it was, some streets had some good-size drifts across them. The snow was plowed into the center of the street, and then a payloader with a large snowblower mounted on the front came along behind and put the snow into trucks, which hauled it to an open field near the river.

While Matthew was out plowing snow, Amber went down to the mobile home and retrieved the envelope with the police photos of his back. At home she said, "Mom, I have something to show you," and handed her mom the envelope.

"This has Matthew's name on it," Susan said. "Are you sure he won't mind?"

"It's okay. They're pictures that show why he was taken out of the foster home and put in the orphanage."

Susan pulled out the letter that was wrapped around the photos and gasped when she saw them. "What monster did this?"

"He still has the scars on his back," Amber said, "and they will always be there."

Susan read the letter. "Nothing was ever done to the man that did this?"

"The lawyers are checking into it," Amber said. "But after all this time, they don't know if there is anything that can be done about it now."

Susan sat down at the table and looked through the photos one by one. John, looking over her shoulder, muttered that the person who did this to Matthew was a coward. How could anyone do this under any circumstances, especially to a child? When they were done, Amber somberly put the photos back in the envelope and returned it to the place Matthew kept it.

CHAPTER

35

When the sun had come up that morning, the snow had tapered off, and so had the wind. By eleven thirty or thereabout, the clouds had started breaking up, and blue sky was peeking through now and then. By one thirty, the sky had cleared, and as the temperature rose, the roads started to melt where they had removed the bulk of the snow. Around three forty-five, Matthew was told by his supervisor to go home.

"We have enough people available now," Bud said, "and we won't be needing you unless something else comes up."

When he got to the mobile home park, the main roads had been cleared. At the trailer he had to shovel the snow off the drive so he could park the truck. He also cleaned out from around his car and cleared off the deck.

When he went in, Amber handed him a cup of coffee and said, "I have some stew on the stove warming up."

He got out of his insulated coveralls and boots. After they ate, they talked about the weather and how the snowstorm was so much heavier than the forecast had led them to expect.

Then Amber told him that she had shown her parents the police photos, and had slipped and told them about the money he had gotten from his inheritance.

Matthew said that was okay. "I don't have any secrets from you or them."

By seven, he was ready for a shower and then would be off to bed. "I will see you in the morning, dear."

But after he had showered, Amber came into the bedroom and sat down on the edge of the bed. They talked until he went to sleep. Only then did she go on home.

CHAPTER

36

Matthew woke up between two thirty and three. He lay there for a while with his stomach growling at him, and finally gave up and headed for the kitchen. After putting together, a sandwich with some milk and cookies, he sat down at the table and noticed through the window that the stars were shining. According to the thermometer, it was warmer out now than when he had gotten home.

Amber came down around seven thirty that morning. He was in the living room, reading the Bible and going over in his mind what he had been hearing the pastor talk about concerning Romans 3:23, "for all have sinned, and come short of the glory of God," and Romans 3:10 where it is written, "there is none righteous, no, not one." He also thought about how it says in the Bible that God showed his love for us by sending his only begotten Son to take our place upon a cross and pay the debt that we could never pay.

Amber fried up some eggs and bacon, and made some toast. While they were eating, she brought up having a Christmas tree.

"I haven't given it any thought," Matthew said. "I am sure we could go and take a look, and see what we might find.

They had picked up an artificial tree that day, along with lights and decorations. Then they went to Hinky Dinky's and on back home.

Back at the mobile home, Amber started putting stuff away in the kitchen while Matthew put the tree together. Her family came down later, and Ann and Angie helped decorate.

Matthew brought up what the pastor had been saying in church, and how his grandmother had talked to him about some of those things but he hadn't really paid that much attention. He knew Grams was very religious, though, and devoted to going to church, so he never wanted to do anything that would be a disappointment to her. For him, it would be like letting her down after all the years that she and his grandpa had raised him when they really didn't have to.

John asked him questions about where he had gone to church growing up and whether he was baptized.

Matthew said that they went to a Methodist church. "My grandmother said, I was sprinkled when I was dedicated to the Lord at infancy. But when I went to the Catholic orphanage, I got sidetracked, and all that had transpired at that time didn't help matters any."

John's next question was most important. "Matthew, do you believe that Jesus is the Son of God and that God raised him from the dead?"

"Oh yes," Matthew said, "I do believe that Jesus is the Son of God and that he was raised from the dead. Especially if he now sits on the right hand of God, as the Bible says."

"Have you ever accepted Christ as your Lord and Savior?"

"That is something I am unsure of," Matthew replied. "I don't remember ever going forward as some have. I always felt glad for those that did, though. I know I am a sinner—I have never really been that good. I've lied, and I've disobeyed at times, and I've been disrespectful to my grandmother at times. Especially when I was much younger.

"But I figured that being a sinner was what I am, and I will try to do my best. The pastor said, and I've read it in the Bible, that all have fallen short of the glory of God, and there is none righteous, no, not one. That's Romans, chapter three, verses twenty-three and ten.

"I have even got out my Strong Concordance, and found that Psalm 14, verses one through three, and Psalm 53, also verses one through three, along with Ecclesiastes 7:20, all say pretty much the same thing."

"It's not by our righteousness, Matthew, but by Jesus's righteousness that we are saved," John said. "We now live in the age of grace.

"In the book of Matthew, chapter eleven, verses twenty-eight through thirty, Christ said, 'Come unto me, all you that labor and are heavy laden, and I will give you rest. Take my yoke upon you, and learn of me; for I am meek and lowly in heart: and you shall find rest unto your souls. For my yoke is easy, and my burden is light.'

"You can't do it on your own, Matthew. Are you laden with sin? We all are. All you have to do is confess your sins and believe on the Lord Jesus Christ, and you will be saved."

Matthew said, "I will give it some more thought."

After they left, Matthew searched the scriptures some more. With the Bible in front of him and a Strong's Concordance laid out on the table beside him, he looked up scriptures and read into the night.

CHAPTER 37

When the Marshalls got back to their place, John said, with frustration in his voice, "He is being stubborn! It is right there in front of him. If he keeps putting off the solution to his need for salvation, I am afraid his heart might get calloused, and he will miss out altogether."

Amber quietly sat at the table, praying with her Bible in front of her.

"O Lord, I so much want to marry Matthew, but you know that will not be possible if he hasn't joined the family of God. Please, Father, move his heart to accept Jesus as his Lord and Savior. The seed has been planted and watered, so please bring forth the increase. In Jesus name, amen."

Susan sat down with a cup of coffee. "You know you can't marry him unless he is saved. For as it is written in Second Corinthians, chapter six, verse fourteen, what do a believer and unbeliever have in common? I know you love him, and so do the rest of us, and I believe he loves you. But he has to get it settled within himself beforehand."

"I will keep praying," Amber said with tears in her eyes.

"As we all will," John said.

On Sunday morning, Amber came down and rode to church with Matthew. She had lost some of her bubbliness because of Matthew's struggle and stubbornness. He commented that she was unusually quiet.

"I'm trying to think of what I might give you for Christmas," she said.

"That is a way off yet, dear."

"What are you going to give me?"

He laughed. "Nice try, dear!"

The Sunday school service gave him some answers to questions he had. By the end of the morning service, the pastor had reiterated that we all are sinners and that God had sent his only begotten Son into the world that the world by him might be saved.

"It says in Acts 4:12 'neither is there salvation in any other: for there is none other name under heaven given among men, whereby we must be saved.'" Then the pastor said, "Today is the day of salvation. You might not have another chance to come forward, whether here or somewhere else. Today is the day you need to make a decision for Christ or against him—and if you don't make one for him, then you just made one against him."

Matthew did not hesitate. He stood up and walked to the front of the church, where he confessed that he was a sinner and asked Christ to be the Lord of his life.

Amber sat in the pew with tears of joy, as did her mother. John lifted up a prayer of thanksgiving to what had just taken place.

After the service they went out to eat in celebration of the wondrous event that had just transpired. Matthew felt like a whole new person, so much had been lifted off his shoulders, and he finally felt forgiveness for those who had abused him.

"I felt sure that you were on the right path," John said. "First Corinthians 3:7 says that one plants a seed and another waters the seed, but only God can bring forth the increase."

"I remember Grandpa saying the same thing," Matthew said, "but I always thought he was talking about planting crops." That caused everyone to laugh.

"The Bible will have much more meaning to you, Matthew, than it ever has before," John said. "Life will not be a bed of roses. In fact, life could become more difficult at times. But always remember that God said, 'I will never leave you, nor forsake you.'"

When Matthew was reading now, the Bible verses did come alive to him and touched his heart and his understanding. It was as if the Bible was speaking directly to him. He had commented to Amber that he felt he was seeing the Word of God for the first time.

"Christ promised us a comforter which is the Holy Spirit, and he will teach us in all things," Amber said, referencing John 14:26.

CHAPTER

38

In the middle of December, Matthew said, "Honey, I know what I want for Christmas."

"Pray tell, what that might be?" Amber said. "Because I already have your Christmas present."

He looked at her and smiled. "You. I want you. Will you marry me?"

Her face lit up, and she practically leaped into his arms. "Yes, yes, yes, I will marry you!"

Matthew talked to her parents, but Susan and John said they could wait until after Amber graduated.

Their daughter protested, "I can be married and still go to school. We can wait on having children."

And so it was that right after the first of the year, her dad walked her down the aisle and placed her hand in Matthew's, thus giving her freely into Matthew's care.

There was no honeymoon. They married on a Saturday, and on Monday Amber returned to school, and Matthew to work.

Matthew's love for Amber continued to grow every day. It was so good to be married to such a wonderful woman.

After six years of marriage, two children had entered the mix, a boy and a girl. The time had come when they needed to find that bigger place they had talked about moving to when Matthew first received his inheritance. They put a down payment on a house and moved out of the trailer, selling it for almost the same price they had paid for it.

But no, their story does not have a fairy tale ending where they live happily ever after, for there is no marriage that ever has had smooth sailing all the time. They had disagreements and sometimes tears, but always they could still truly say to each other, "I am upset with you, but I love you and always will."

The promise from up above is to trust in Jesus

Christ, the very Son of God, and you too will have life everlasting. It is written in Hebrews 9:27–28:

> And as it is appointed unto men once to die, but after this the judgement: So Christ was once offered to bear the sins of many; and unto them that look for him shall he appear the second time without sin unto salvation.

Printed in the United States
by Baker & Taylor Publisher Services

Printed in the United States
by Baker & Taylor Publisher Services